A Ladybird Book
Series 561

This is a book about the Romans, what kind of people they were and their way of life. It tells of their homes, their often cruel forms of entertainment, their beliefs and superstitions and the gods they worshipped.

It also tells of their great empire, and how widely differing peoples were brought under Roman rule.

CONTENTS

Great Civilisations
ROME

by CLARENCE GREIG, B.A. (Dunelm), M.A. (Oxon).
with illustrations by JORGE NUNEZ

Ladybird Books Loughborough

Our Roman heritage

Few people have not heard of the Romans. In 500 BC they were simple shepherds, living in the centre of Italy. By the time of the birth of Jesus Christ they were masters of an empire that stretched all around the Mediterranean Sea.

The Romans were great soldiers and established a reputation for success on the battlefields. They also built fine roads, aqueducts and fortresses, all of which helped to bring about peace in troublesome places. When the Roman soldiers established order in a province, then others – farmers, shopkeepers, men, women and children, Romans and non-Romans – went there to start a new life. But even though such people went to live in a province they lived under Roman government and Roman laws. Romans brought many different nations to live together happily. To do this they had to be hard and cruel, but they believed that the gods had ordered them to be like that. They thought that they had been allowed to build up their great empire because the gods wished them to do so.

There are many places in Europe today where you can see remains of the Roman Empire. For example, in Britain you can still walk along parts of the wall built by the Roman emperor, Hadrian. In the south of France there is the famous Roman aqueduct, the Pont du Gard, which helped to bring water to the city of Nimes. The Romans also left us a different sort of heritage; their language was called Latin and many of the books and speeches they wrote are still studied today. Some modern languages are based on Latin, such as French, Spanish and, particularly, Italian.

Early Rome

The Roman writer, Livy, told us that there were many reasons why the gods and men decided to build the city of Rome where they did. The city was built on seven hills so that its position was very healthy. The River Tiber could carry the farm produce down to Rome from the neighbouring countryside. The Romans could use the Tiber to import goods from abroad. Livy also wrote that the site of the city was sixteen miles inland – just near enough to the coast to use the sea, but far enough away to be safe from pirates. The city was in the middle of Italy, and Italy was in the middle of the Mediterranean. Clearly, he thought, that was what the gods must have wanted.

What Livy said is only partly true. The site of the city was not particularly well-chosen. The area is not very healthy, the River Tiber very often floods, and is difficult for the passage of ships because it often silts up.

The first buildings on the seven hills of Rome were shepherds' huts. These were little round houses made of turf and timber. There are shelters like these for shepherds in Italy today. According to a legend, two brothers, Romulus and Remus, founded the city of Rome. They were twins and were said to have been brought up by a wolf. They started to build the city together, but they were very jealous of each other. After a quarrel, Romulus became so angry that he killed his brother.

There are many other legends about early Rome. Like the stories of King Arthur or Robin Hood and others, some may be based on facts but the rest were just imagined.

Horatius

One of the legends of Rome is the story of Horatius. Tarquinius Superbus (Tarquin the Proud), the last of Rome's seven kings, was so cruel that the citizens forced him from the city. Tarquinius took refuge with the Etruscans, who decided to attack Rome and put their friend back on the throne.

As the Etruscan army approached, the Romans left their farms and moved into the city. The only weak point in their defences was a wooden bridge that led across the River Tiber into the heart of Rome. By good fortune, the bridge was guarded on that day by Horatius Cocles, a soldier of great courage. On seeing his own comrades running away from the Etruscans, he tried to stop them, but without success.

It was a desperate situation; if Rome was to be saved he had to act quickly. He ordered as many men as possible to destroy the end of the bridge nearest Rome, while he himself stood alone at the other end facing the Etruscans. He stood, one man, sword in hand, against an army. Two other Roman soldiers were so shamed by his courage that they joined him on the bridge. All three fought side by side until Horatius sent the other two back.

The Etruscans attacked him in even greater numbers, but Horatius refused to abandon his post until the Romans behind him had cut down the supports of the bridge. When the timbers crashed into the river, Horatius offered a prayer to the river god, Tiber, asking for his protection. Then he plunged into the water, still wearing his armour, and swam to safety.

Horatius' bravery saved Rome from the Etruscans, and from a return to the rule of the hated king, Tarquinius Superbus.

Hannibal

During its long history, the city of Rome and its people were attacked by many enemies. One of the greatest of these was Hannibal. Hannibal lived at Carthage, a powerful city on the north coast of Africa. Before he was born, the Romans and Carthaginians had fought a war over the island of Sicily, which lay between Italy and Carthage.

Hannibal's father had often reminded him of the way Rome had defeated the Carthaginians. Hannibal promised his father that he would avenge this defeat. To make his attempt he gathered together a huge army at Carthage – ships, soldiers, cavalry, men, horses, elephants and baggage animals – crossed the Mediterranean from Africa into Spain, and marched through Spain and Gaul. From Gaul they crossed the Alps into Italy.

Within two years of arriving in Italy, he had defeated the Romans in four battles, causing heavy losses. In the last battle, the Carthaginians killed 25,000 and captured 10,000 of the best Roman troops. After this battle Hannibal was urged to attack Rome. "Within five days you will feast in the city", said a friend who tried to persuade him.

However, Hannibal did not march on Rome. Instead, he spent the next fourteen years in the south of Italy, harassing the Romans but never quite defeating them. Even so, it was a tremendous achievement for the Carthaginians to remain in their enemy's land for as long as sixteen years.

Finally the Romans invaded North Africa and forced Hannibal to return home to defend his own city, Carthage. When he reached Carthage his fortunes changed. The Romans had at last found an able general of their own, Publius Scipio. Hannibal lost the battle. He fled to Bithynia and there he committed suicide. It was a sad end to a great enemy of Rome.

Caratacus

During their campaign against Hannibal, the Romans fought in Spain, Africa, Gaul and Sicily. After their victory, they had to decide what to do with these places and how to treat the inhabitants. They decided to make Spain and Africa Roman provinces. A province was a territory to which a governor was sent from Rome. He was responsible to the Romans for the province and ruled it with the help of Roman soldiers. The governor and the army established law and order, which attracted merchants, farmers and others from the homeland.

The decision on Spain and Africa was not an easy one to take. Hitherto, the Romans had been unwilling to govern in other lands, and for many years after the defeat of Hannibal they tried not to get too involved with affairs outside their own country. This was particularly true of the eastern shores of the Mediterranean, where there were many Greek cities. These cities had quarrelled and fought each other for centuries.

Around the western half of the Mediterranean there were very few cities before the Romans came. The Romans wanted to build cities, but first they had to defeat those enemies who stood in their way. Some of Rome's enemies fought hard before being overcome.

Later, when the emperor Claudius ordered an invasion of Britain in AD 43, one famous Briton, Caratacus, resisted stubbornly for nine years before he was captured and sent to Rome in chains with his wife and brother. There the emperor Claudius had him led through the streets in a great triumphal procession. Although Caratacus seemed a rough barbarian, he was nevertheless a king and he behaved like one. Claudius was so impressed with the dignity of his captive that he did not have him killed. Caratacus was allowed to live in Rome, an honoured enemy.

Hadrian's Wall

The Roman Empire was surrounded by many barbarian tribes such as the Parthians in the east and the Germans in the north. The Romans had to protect themselves against these tribes and they did so in many ways. Sometimes the Romans used their legions in battle and sometimes they made friends with the barbarian kings to avoid trouble on their frontiers. Occasionally they actually built a frontier fortification and stationed soldiers on it. The best known example was the great wall which was built in Britain on the orders of the emperor Hadrian. The wall stretched for eighty Roman miles, roughly between what is now Newcastle and Carlisle.

It was built between AD 122 and AD 128 by three Roman legions. Starting from the east side of the country, the first forty-five miles were built in stone, the other thirty-five in turf. The wall itself is one of three lines of defence:

1. A ditch 27ft. wide, 9ft. deep, in front of the stone wall.
2. The wall itself, 10ft. broad and 16ft. high.
3. South of the wall, a great ditch called the vallum. The earth from the vallum was piled in two mounds, one on each side, and the distance between these mounds was 120ft.

Along the length of the wall were built milecastles and turrets. Soon after it was started, the original plan was changed and sixteen forts were added to the wall. The soldiers who lived in the forts and manned the wall did not come from the Roman legions. They were called 'auxiliaries' and came from Dalmatia, Asturia and Thrace. These auxiliaries were not considered to be as valuable as the legions and it was thought to be no great loss if they were killed fighting Rome's enemies.

The land of Italy

On a map, Italy looks like a long boot, with the toe facing North Africa and the top towards Switzerland. Running almost its whole length is a mountain chain called the Appennines. Nearly three-quarters of the land is made up of either mountains or hills. In the north is the great barrier of the Alps. There are over 2,000 miles of coastline, but few good harbours, which may explain why the Romans were poor sailors.

In early times, many different races of people lived in Italy. The Romans were only one of them. Even when the Romans became masters of all Italy, the others still thought of themselves as separate from the Romans. The Samnites and Lucanians were not Roman, just as the Welsh and Scots are not English.

The Romans were good farmers. Being a practical people they made the most of the land in which they lived. They planted vines and made wine; they grew cereal crops including corn, olives and many other fruits and vegetables. Although they had large flocks of sheep and herds of cattle, the sheep and cattle were used to produce wool and leather. The Romans ate very little meat, even though they fished and hunted game. Corn was preferred as their basic diet.

They tried to be self-sufficient by living off the land around them. This was important, because transporting goods by road in Roman times was very expensive. Those who lived in the middle of Italy had to learn to manage with what they had.

Much of Italy was made up of small towns on the sides of hills, with farmland below. The farmland was valued highly by the Romans. They loved the country-side and wrote about it in their poetry. In farming a man had to work hard and use his hands. This way of life ideally suited the Romans.

Roman houses

Roman houses were different from the houses in which we live today. There was more privacy, for although the fronts of the houses came right up to the pavement, there were few windows in the outside walls. Most houses were only one storey high. The poor people lived in blocks of flats called *insulae* (islands).

The house of a rich man had two courtyards; the first was called the *atrium* and was the most important part of the house. Around the atrium were the main rooms, the bedrooms, the dining room and the study. In the centre of the atrium was a shallow square pool, under an opening in the roof which let in light and rain.

There was very little furniture in the atrium, usually no more than a small marble table and a bronze chest for the family treasures. In one corner was the *lararium* (altar) before which all the family, including the slaves, would worship. In it were kept the little gods that protected the house. The picture opposite shows a Roman family worshipping at their lararium.

The decorations of the atrium were interesting. There were large panels usually coloured red, orange or blue. Sometimes the walls were painted with pictures from well known myths, such as Narcissus falling in love with himself. Sometimes the pictures showed a stage and a theatre, with masks, columns and garlands.

In the second courtyard were the garden, the kitchens and the slaves' quarters. A Roman garden was very formal, with statues and fountains and carefully laid out borders full of small shrubs.

The slaves of the house were part of the *familia* (family), but belonged to the lower end of the social order. They lived in their master's fine house but some slaves were really little more than necessary parts of the equipment. It was convenient for the Romans to have their slaves living with them.

The city of Rome

Because the Romans built a great empire, it might be expected that the city of Rome would have been properly planned; but it was not. Until the victorious Roman generals brought back money and tribute from their conquests, Rome had few fine buildings.

The first emperor, Augustus (who died in AD 14), tried to make Rome look like the capital of a great empire. He boasted that, on becoming emperor, he had found a city made of brick, but on his death he would leave a city made of marble. Augustus built temples and completed the great forum started by Julius Caesar. He also persuaded citizens to give money for new public buildings.

The emperors did not build houses for the poor of Rome. There were no houses built by the government, as are our council houses. The Romans were quite content to live in poor conditions and enjoy sharing splendid public buildings. Living in such a warm climate, they spent far more time out of doors than we do.

Shown below is part of a list which gives some of the attractions of Rome in AD 354:

Bibliothecae XXVIII	- 28 libraries
Pontes VII	- 7 bridges
Montes VII	- 7 hills
Campi VIII	- 8 large parks
Fora XI	- 11 Forums
Basilicae X	- 10 Basilicas
Thermae XI	- 11 sets of public baths
Aquae XVIIII	- 19 Aqueducts
Viae XXVIIII	- 29 roads

The list gives no indication of the size and majesty of the buildings. For example, the public baths built by the Emperor Diocletian could hold 3,000 people. The picture opposite shows a part of the Roman Forum.

The Great Fire of Rome

In the summer of AD 64, a great fire broke out in the city of Rome. The fire lasted nine days and destroyed nearly three-quarters of the city. Many citizens lost their lives; thousands more were made homeless.

The emperor at this time was Nero. He helped those who had lost their homes by building shelters for them in his gardens in the city. He also introduced new building regulations. All new houses had to be made from materials that would not catch fire quickly. In addition every Roman had to have fire-fighting equipment in his house.

Because Nero's palace had been burnt down, he decided to build another one. The new palace was so splendid that it was called the *Aurea Domus* – the Golden House. In the entrance hall stood a 120ft. high statue of Nero. Some of the rooms were decorated with gold and jewels, and the dining room had a ceiling covered with ivory. In the grounds were three colonnades, an enormous lake, parks, fields and vineyards. Wild animals ran in its woods.

When the poor people of Rome heard of the wonders of Nero's new palace, they became very angry. They declared that Nero had set fire to the city so that he could find land on which to build his new palace. Nero felt that he had to find someone to blame for starting the fire, so he blamed the Christians. They were arrested, and some were put in the arena. They were then wrapped in skins of wild animals and torn to pieces by savage dogs. Others were nailed to crosses and covered with tar before being burnt alive at night as human torches. The terrible deaths of the Christians served no purpose; the Romans still believed that Nero started the fire.

The Colosseum

The Colosseum is one of the biggest buildings to survive from Roman times. Its real name was the Amphitheatrum Flavium, but it was known as the Colosseum because it was built on the site of a 'colossal' statue of Nero.

The amphitheatre took ten years to build; when completed it had four storeys and could hold 50,000 people. In the centre was an oval-shaped arena, where gladiators killed animals – or each other. This arena could also be filled with water to stage realistic sea battles, often between many galleys. Around the arena was a high wall which separated the gladiators from the spectators. The front rows of seats were reserved for important Romans and there was a special box for the emperor and his family.

The Colosseum played an important part in Roman life. Once the emperor Trajan put on 'games' there for 123 consecutive days. The spectators saw 11,000 animals and 10,000 gladiators put to death.

Each large town had its own amphitheatre, usually the biggest building in the town. The amphitheatre at Pompeii could hold an audience of 20,000, which was almost the whole adult population. Many of the Romans found it entertaining and amusing to watch others die. The *lanistae*, who were responsible for training the gladiators, taught them how to die nobly. Dying well was considered to be an art and was the duty of every gladiator. The attitude of the Romans to them can be explained only by the fact that the gladiators were slaves, and were therefore considered to be animals like the tigers and lions they fought.

The Circus Maximus

The Romans liked watching chariot racing. The biggest building in Rome was the Circus Maximus, where the chariot racing was held. This building could hold 350,000 people – a third of the total population of Rome at that time.

The Circus Maximus was a magnificent race track. It had two parallel sides and semicircular ends. A wall ran down the middle and at the ends of the wall were turning points.

Each race was run over seven laps and there were many sorts of races. Some chariots were drawn by four horses, others by six, eight or even twelve. To drive even a four-horsed chariot needed a great deal of skill. The charioteers wore leather protective helmets and were dressed in tunics of either red, white, blue or green. They were as popular then as footballers are today. A tombstone of a charioteer reads:

"Here lies G. Apuleius Diocles, charioteer from the Red Stable. He was born in Spain. When he died he was 42 years, 7 months and 23 days old. He had also ridden in the Green and White Stables. For 24 years he raced chariots in 4257 races and won 1462 times. With each of 9 of his horses he won a hundred races, and with one horse, two hundred."

Many aspects of the Circus Maximus had a religious significance. Its shape was the same shape as the Romans believed the heavens to be; the twelve gates represented the twelve months; the four-horse chariots, the four seasons. Before the shows began, statues of the gods were carried along in a procession and priests made sacrifices.

The Senate

The men who ruled Rome were *nobiles* – noble men. The nobiles governed the Roman world and were the most important people in it. They thought that they had inherited the right to rule. Their families had become 'noble' by being elected to the highest office in the land – one of the two consuls. If a man's father and grandfather had been consul, he would expect to be the same. Although they were mostly wealthy landowners, nobiles made much more money when they went out to act as governors of the provinces.

A nobilis needed many friends. Sometimes a son inherited his father's friends and enemies. A Roman nobilis often made friends by helping people. He might defend them in court or prosecute one of their enemies. He might lend them money or arrange the marriage of a daughter to a rich man. He acted as their *patronus* (patron) by giving his influential support to them. They were his *clientes* – which meant 'friends', rather than the modern term 'clients'.

Nobiles also acted on behalf of kings, princes, cities and whole communities. If a foreign king had a problem with the Romans, he solved it by asking his patron in Rome to speak for him in the Senate or get the support of other senators. To be successful and influential, a Roman had to be of noble birth, a good army officer and a persuasive speaker in the Senate and law-courts.

The nobiles had great power. When Gnaius Pompeius returned to Rome from the provinces, he had as friends the most important people in the eastern half of the Empire; he had also come to own a large part of it.

The nobiles were always thinking of their own interests. What they meant by *libertas* (freedom), was freedom to pursue their own ambitions. This attitude was one of the causes of the civil wars.

The emperors

Julius Caesar was murdered because he wanted to be King of Rome. After his death a bitter war broke out between the armies of two rivals for his position. The war was won by Caesar's nephew, Octavian, who triumphed over Marcus Antonius and the Egyptian Queen, Cleopatra. Octavian realised that the only way to solve the troubles of the Roman Empire was for one man to rule. There needed to be *pax et princeps* (peace and government by one man).

Octavian was a shrewd politician. He realised that everyone had to help in bringing about settled conditions. He had to turn to good use all the restless energy, all the anger, all the pride of the Roman nobiles; and in this he succeeded. He also changed his name to Augustus – the hallowed one. As the first emperor he worked hard, and was loved by many. He was also feared by those closest to him, particularly the senators. There were plots and intrigues against Augustus as there were against his successors. The Emperor was seldom popular with the Senate – or even with his own family. However, he kept the common people happy, and he was liked by them.

Some emperors were popular because they worked so hard. The emperor Vespasian, who built the Colosseum*, got up before dawn to read his letters; he also spent a long time listening to endless requests from the poor. Although he earned the respect of the Romans by his wisdom and ability, he also earned a reputation for extreme meanness. Even at his funeral, his speech and gestures were mocked by the chief clown to the court. Pretending to be Vespasian, the clown protested that he was shocked at the cost of his own burial!

The fourth storey of the Colosseum was added after Vespasian's death by his son Domitian.

Pliny

Pliny's Roman name was Gaius Plinius Caecilius Secundus. He was born at Comum, a small town in the north of Italy, and lived between AD 61 and AD 114. We know a great deal about him because he wrote many letters which we can still read.

Pliny came from a well known Italian family. His uncle had been admiral of the Roman fleet based at Misenum, near Naples. Although the Roman navy was not as important as the Roman army, Pliny's uncle, as an admiral, was a powerful man. It was from his uncle's villa near Naples that Pliny, as a young man, watched the eruption of Vesuvius.

Pliny had a distinguished career under four emperors. Towards the end of his life he became consul and was sent out by the emperor Trajan to govern the Roman province of Bithynia, which was on the edge of the Black Sea. Probably it was here that he died.

Pliny was rich; he owned four villas near Rome, and several more along the lake at Comum and elsewhere. But although a wealthy landowner, he preferred to spend most of his life in the city of Rome. Besides becoming one of the most famous orators of his day, he was also a great lawyer and one of the best known writers. He was trusted and respected. From his letters we can see that he claims to be a kind and humane master to his many slaves. Some were freed after faithful service; others were looked after when they became ill. Although careful with money, he generously helped to set up a library and a school in the city of Comum. In his will there were instructions for a set of public baths to be built; money was left for a hundred of his freedmen and for a feast for the townsfolk. Pliny was generous and kind-hearted, but his weakness was that he liked people to know about his good deeds.

The poor in Rome

Juvenal lived in the city of Rome just after the time when the Colosseum was built. He was a rich man who wrote poems about life in Rome. In one of them a poor man explains why he has to leave Rome. This is part of the translation of the poem and it gives a vivid picture:

"I am a poor man. I cannot stop in Rome any more. An honest man cannot make a living here. The city is full of Greeks who lie and cheat. They can do anything they like. If you tell a Greek to go to hell, he'll get there.

You ought to pity us poor Romans. We are the ones who are suffering. Everyone laughs at me, my cloak is torn, my toga is dirty and I've got holes in my shoes. Some people don't know how expensive it is to live in Rome. A poor man can only afford to rent a room in the attics of the great blocks of flats. And what happens when there is a fire? The poor man in his attic is the last to know. If a rich man's great house is burnt down, all his friends come with presents to help him start again. That doesn't happen to the poor. Life is so unfair.

I cannot get to sleep at nights. I have to live in the noisiest parts of Rome, where traffic all night long keeps me awake. When I get up in the morning to visit a wealthy friend for a loan of some money or a little food, life is difficult. I try to dash through the streets to get there before anyone else, but the streets are all crowded. Someone digs me with his elbow, someone else hits me on the head with a great pole he is carrying. The soldiers tread on my toes and my legs get filthy with the mud from the streets. If I go out at night some bully who is drunk, attacks me and beats me.

It is just not worth living in the city of Rome – if you are poor. I am emigrating – to a nice little Greek city in the south of Italy!"

Roman religion

A Roman who was religious worshipped many different gods. They included:

1. **The gods of noble families** – the important gods such as Jupiter, the father of gods and men. The Romans called him *'Juppiter Optimus Maximus'* – the best and biggest. His wife was *Juno* and his brother *Neptunus*, God of the Sea. These gods were worshipped in the great temples throughout the Empire by public priests and officials at public ceremonies. The picture opposite shows the Pantheon in Rome which contained many statues of these gods.

2. **Gods of the family and home** – the *Lares* and *Penates* – the gods who protected the family. Most Romans had a shrine in their house where small statues of these gods, six or seven inches high, were kept.

3. **Gods of places.** Like Old Father Thames, *Tiber*, the god of their river, was thought of as a person. The nymph *Coventina* was worshipped at her well near Hadrian's Wall.

4. **Gods of things** – such as *Fortuna* – god of luck, *Pietas* – god of duty, *Concordia* – god of working together in peace.

5. **The emperor gods.** The emperors were thought to be bringers of peace and prosperity, so all emperors, living and dead, were worshipped as gods, as were their families.

A Roman worshipped all these gods at different times. His religion involved making a bargain. 'The God will do something for me and when he has done it, I will do something for him.' After his wish had been fulfilled, he set up an altar to let everyone know the God had kept his word. Here is an example:

C. Tetius Veturius Micinus . . . fulfilled his vow and set up this altar because he killed a splendid wild boar which no-one could capture.

The god Mithras

Mithras was a Persian god, who was worshipped at first in the East and later all over the Roman world. His worshippers included many merchants and soldiers. Very often altars and temples to him have been found near army camps and harbours. The Mithraic religion had many things in common with Christianity. Like the birth of Jesus Christ, the birth of Mithras was said to have been a miracle. It was also said that shepherds went to see the infant Mithras.

Mithras was a complex figure. He favoured the good and acted as a kind of messenger between the gods and men. In some stories he is a friend of the sun-god, and in others he *is* the sun-god. On many altars he is described as *Mithras Sol Invictus* (Mithras the sun that cannot be conquered).

The worship of Mithras was a religion of mystery. The temples dedicated to him were made to look like small dark caves with low roofs. At the entrance to them stood two statues. One was called *Cautes* and held a torch pointing upwards, which symbolized light and life. Opposite stood *Cautopates*, holding a torch pointing down, symbolizing darkness and death. At the far end of each temple was a large altar-piece which showed the god Mithras killing a large bull.

The followers of Mithras were divided into seven grades. Special ceremonies were held when they entered each one. We know some of the names of the grades – *leo* (lion), *miles* (soldier), *corax* (raven) – but we do not know any details of what took place at the ceremonies. Starting at the lowest, a follower could rise through the seven grades until he had reached the highest of them.

In many countries the remains of temples to Mithras can still be seen. The illustration opposite shows a reconstruction of one such temple which was found at Carrawburgh, near Hadrian's Wall.

The Christians

Gaius Plinius Secundus was sent to govern the Roman province of Bithynia. Later he wrote this letter to the emperor about one of his problems:

"Pliny to the emperor Trajan,

I write to you, Sir, because I do not know what to do. It is about the Christians. I have never been to a court where Christians have been put on trial, so I do not know how they are to be punished or what I should do with them.

This is what I have done so far. When people are brought before me, as Governor, and charged with being Christians, I ask them, first of all, if they are. If they say "Yes", I ask them a second and a third time, warning them that they will be severely punished if they say "Yes". If they still say "Yes", I order them to be killed. Those who are Roman citizens, I have sent to you at Rome. Those who say that they are not Christians, I let go, but only after they have prayed to our gods, offered wine and incense to your statue and cursed the name of Christ. Real Christians will not do any of these things.

Some who were Christians years ago, but have now given it up, say that all they did was to meet before dawn and sing hymns to Christ as if he were a god. Later in the day they would meet again and break bread. I tortured two slave girls who were Christian priestesses and they said this was true.

I would welcome your advice because this is a serious problem. There are many Christians in towns, villages and the countryside, who have become infected with this mad disease."

Forecasting the future

The Romans are said to have been very superstitious, but this is not quite fair to them. It would be better to say that they developed a series of skills which they thought would help to tell them what was going to happen. If they foresaw something bad, they could take action and try to avoid it. To do this they used the world around them for evidence. At Rome, there were priests called *augures*, who tried to foretell the future using the following methods:

They studied the sky, and in particular, lightning and thunder.

They watched the flight of birds, listened to their cries and looked at the ways they ate their food. They also watched animals to see what they did.

The priests also took into account anything unusual; for example, if they saw a dog carrying a human hand in the street, this would have a special meaning to them.

To be sure that he had the correct interpretation of the signs, the ordinary Roman had to go to an expert. There were many experts who were not honest and who would say things in the hope that they themselves would benefit. One of Pliny's enemies, M. Atilius Regulus, was one of them. He was what the Romans called a *captator* – a catcher or fortune-hunter.

Regulus wanted an old lady, called Verania, to leave him part of her fortune when she died. To achieve his purpose he visited her to frighten her when she was sick. After asking her the day and hour when she was born, Regulus pretended to do some sums, counting on his fingers and mumbling to himself. Then he sat and did not say a word. At last he whispered, "Verania, you are in terrible danger, but it will pass." Finally he made a sacrifice and inspected it closely. The old lady was so frightened by all this that she altered her will and left Regulus a fortune.

Establishing peace

The Roman poet Virgil, who lived at the same time as Christ, wrote a poem about an early Roman hero called Aeneas. In one part of the poem Aeneas went down into the Underworld. Here he met the ghost of his father. His father looked into the future and told him what kind of people the Romans would become. This is part of what he said:

"Others will be able to hammer out bronze better than you can, and make it have the feel of life. From hard marble they will also be able to bring forth faces that seem alive. Others will be better lawyers than the Romans and know more about the stars. All that I can believe. But what you should also remember, if you are to be a true Roman, is this. Rule over the peoples of the world; let them live by your command. Make them live peaceful lives. Be kind to those whom you have defeated, but crush utterly any who are too proud to accept your rule. These are to be your skills."

It is clear from the poem that Virgil was making a contrast between the Greeks and Romans. The Greeks were artistic, skilful sculptors, lawyers and astronomers. What the poet did not mention was that the Greeks did not know how to live together happily. When reading Virgil's comments about the Romans, it is important to understand what he meant. He did not say that they were not artistic; he said that the Romans excelled at another kind of art – the art of government. No others knew more about establishing peace among the warring tribes of other lands.

When the Romans did secure peace in a part of their world, they often celebrated by setting up a triumphal arch. You can still see the arch of Titus, which was set up in Rome to celebrate the Emperor Titus' defeat of the Jews and the capture of Jerusalem.

TRANSLATION OF INSCRIPTION

The Senate and People of Rome dedicate this arch to the God Emperor Titus Vespasianus Augustus son of the God Emperor Vespasian.

Tiberius Claudius Cogidubnus

The Romans built a great empire, but even they could not hope to rule it by themselves; they had to have the assistance of the people they had conquered.

One of those who helped the Romans was Tiberius Claudius Cogidubnus. He was a Celt who lived on the south coast of Britain, near Southampton. What is known about him comes mostly from this translation of a remarkable inscription on a stone slab found near Chichester: "To Neptune and Minerva, for the welfare of the Roman emperor and his family, the college of smiths and its members built this temple out of their own money. Clemens the son of Pudentinus gave the land. The temple was built on the authority of Tiberius Claudius Cogidubnus, king and legatus Augusti in Britain."

Cogidubnus was a barbarian who was made a Roman citizen by the emperor Claudius. Cogidubnus worked for the Romans and they made him a king. The inscription was on a temple built to two gods – Neptune, God of the Sea, and Minerva, Goddess of War.

Twenty years before this, another temple had been built by the emperor Claudius at Camulodunum – Colchester. This was the temple that Boudicca attacked and destroyed when she rebelled against the Romans.

Tiberius Claudius Cogidubnus was made *legatus Augusti* – second governor of the province. In some ways he was like Herod Agrippa, who helped the Romans control his people, the Jews. Herod, too, was rewarded by the Romans.

At Fishbourne, near Chichester, are the remains of a splendid Roman palace. It had tessellated floors as in the picture opposite. The palace may have been built by the Romans for Cogidubnus. A Roman writer called him *fidissimus*, most faithful. That was the highest praise a Roman could give. Boudicca and Caratacus would have thought of Cogidubnus as a traitor.

Slaves and citizens

Roman citizens had three names or more, like Gaius Salvius Liberalis Nonius Bassus, who was a wealthy Roman. Spartacus was a slave; he had one name, just as today, animals like cats and dogs have only one name. Slaves were not thought of as human beings, but as useful objects to be bought and sold. People made a living by selling slaves, in the same way as people these days make a living by selling cars.

Slaves were important to the Romans. At that time there were no machines, and their slaves did much of the work that machines do for us today. In modern life we have dishwashers, vacuum cleaners, automatic cookers, tractors, cars, television, radio and the cinema. A rich Roman had many different sorts of slaves. When he travelled, he used six or eight strong slaves to carry him on a litter; if he wanted to be entertained a slave might read to him, another might sing for him, or yet another might dance for him. One Roman lady kept a whole company of actors, all slaves, because she liked watching plays.

Slaves were employed in many different ways. They were also treated differently according to the work they did. In the picture opposite you can see three people. The Roman lady, the wife of a rich Roman citizen, is seated in the middle buying perfume. Behind her is her maid, a little slave girl who is quite well dressed. The boy selling the perfume is a slave from the perfume shop. He is not as well dressed as the slave girl because he is not a house slave. He lives and works in a perfume factory. Those who were treated the best were the house slaves who attended to the personal needs of their master or mistress. Worst treated were those slaves who had to work on the farms.

The masters of the world

The Romans were a proud people, as we can see from their impressive public buildings and monuments. They were also supremely confident in everything they did. This confidence was strengthened by the belief that the gods were on their side.

They were also stubbornly determined. Their armies might suffer several defeats but, in the end, the Romans won. They believed that they were bringing peace to the world by forcing other nations into the Roman Empire. We would regard this as cruel, but they did not. To us, a symbol of peace might be a dove carrying an olive branch; to the Romans it might be a statue (like that shown opposite) of the soldier emperor Augustus, calm but firm, imposing order on the Empire.

Although the Empire was a Roman empire, with Roman laws, customs and government, the conquered peoples were allowed to keep many of their own ways and customs. The Romans also absorbed customs and ideas from the people they conquered. They believed in a clear distinction between citizens and slaves, yet some slaves were freed and their children became full Roman citizens. Thus, many Roman citizens were themselves descended from slaves.

Although proud and cruel, the Romans were also artistic. They regarded the writing of poetry and prose as important. Pliny, a wealthy politician and governor, enjoyed writing more than anything else. Lucretius wrote a scientific treatise in poetry and Virgil wrote a poem about keeping bees. The Romans did not find this odd. Horatius, a Roman poet, said of his poems, "I have built a monument which will last much longer than any building or work of art."